Teach Them to Your Children

To my father, whose masterful storytelling
sparked my early interest in writing;

To my mother, who encouraged me for years
to complete this project;

To my husband and sons, the three most precious gifts
God has given me.

SECOND PRINTING
COPYRIGHT © 2006-2007 THE VISION FORUM, INC.
All Rights Reserved

"Where there is no vision, the people perish." (Proverbs 29:18)

The Vision Forum, Inc.
4719 Blanco Rd., San Antonio, Texas 78212
www.visionforum.com

ISBN-10 0-9787559-5-2
ISBN-13 978-0-9787559-5-9

Illustrated by Lori Hood Sanford, who may be contacted at
125 Penn View Drive, P.O. Box 970, Penns Creek, PA 17862
or by calling (570) 837-3033.

Book Design by Shannon G. Moeller

PRINTED IN THE UNITED STATES OF AMERICA

Teach Them to Your Children

An Alphabet of Biblical Poems, Verses, and Stories

By Sarah Wean
Illustrated by Lori Hood Sanford

THE VISION FORUM, INC.
SAN ANTONIO, TEXAS

Always in all things,
Whether work or play or school,
Give your all as to the Lord—
May this always be your rule.

"And now, to reveal my masterpiece! Drum roll, please!" Aaron's siblings made the appropriate drumming noises as he dramatically swept the blanket off the table. Appreciative oohs and aahs followed. "Aaron, I think that is the finest Lego fortress you have built yet," his mother exclaimed, "and it should be—after all the hours you've spent working on it! Your effort is evident." "Thank you!" Aaron beamed. "And now children, I must bring this ceremony to a close by asking you to comply with your father's request that you all finish breaking down and stacking the boxes left in the garage from our move." Aaron groaned. "Aaron," his mother said, "why did you cheerfully spend hours building your fortress but now complain about your work?" "Because I like Legos, Mother. They're fun!" "I know, Aaron," his mother began, "but the Lord asks us to do everything as if we were doing it for Him, and not just what we like to do. How would you have responded if *Jesus* had asked you to take

care of the boxes?" Aaron's eyes grew wide. "I would have said, 'Yes, sir!' and done it right away." "Well," his mother replied, "if we're to do everything as if for the Lord, then you can look at any task you're given as if He Himself has asked you to do it. Now why don't you try to apply what we've just talked about to the boxes and see how it goes." An hour later, Aaron triumphantly re-entered the house with his siblings in tow and exclaimed, "We're done!" His mother poked her head into the garage and was amazed at the orderly, perfectly stacked piles of flattened boxes she found. "Excellent job, children! I have no corrections to give. Aaron, how did it go?" "It made all the difference, Mother, to do my task as if I were directly obeying the Lord and wanting to please Him. It was still hard work, but my attitude was different. I'll try to do all my tasks like this from now on."

And whatever you do, do it heartily, as to the Lord and not to men.
(Colossians 3:23)

Be the one to first forgive
Or ask for forgiveness to bring peace,
Show to others humble love
And you'll find that strivings cease.

"Bethany!" Sarah exclaimed as she walked into the bedroom that she and her little sister shared. "Look what you did to my Liberty doll! She's ruined!" Bethany's face clouded over. "I was just trying to give her bangs a trim like Mama does to you." Sarah took one last look at her doll's now-bare forehead and the pile of doll hair on the floor at her sister's feet before stomping down the hall. "I'm telling!" she yelled over her shoulder. "Mom, guess what Bethany has done now..." Sarah started as she entered the kitchen, but her mother stopped her. "Sarah, this is the fourth time you've been in here today with a complaint about Bethany. Honey, I want you to think about something. Christ blessed those who made peace. I know it is much easier to get angry with your little sister when she upsets you, but Christ says that those who make the harder choice to offer selfless love and

forgiveness will be called sons of God. Ask the Lord to show you how to be a peacemaker with Bethany." Sarah turned slowly from her mother and with a sigh walked back to her room. After pausing outside the door for a minute to pray and calm down, she entered. Bethany sat where Sarah had left her, waiting with anxious eyes for another scornful rebuke. "Bethany—" Sarah took a deep breath. "Would you forgive me for getting angry with you? That was very wrong of me. It's just a doll, but you're my sister." Bethany's eyes widened in surprise and then filled with tears. "I'm sorry for ruining your Liberty doll," she sniffled. "I'll give you my Evangeline doll instead." "No, don't do that," Sarah said smiling. "Instead, why don't you help me make a hat for her to wear until her hair grows out!" Both girls laughed.

Blessed are the peacemakers, for they shall be called sons of God. (Matthew 5:9)

Children, mind your parents
And obey in heart and deed,
Doing as the Bible tells you
And the Lord will be well pleased.

"Could I go over to Nicole's house, Mom?" Katie asked. "They just put up their new swing set and she wants me to come try it. Pleeease!" "No, dear," her mother answered. "I'd rather you wait until I can go with you, and I can't do that today, okay?" "Okay," Katie sighed. Then she thought of another idea. "Can I go for a bike ride instead?" "Yes, I think that would be fine," her mother said, smiling. "Why don't you take your brother with you, too." "Yes Ma'am!" Katie cheered as she bounced out the door. A few minutes later, Katie and Jeremy began to make their usual lap around the block when Nicole's house suddenly came into view, along with her big new swing set. Katie slowed her bike as she passed the driveway. "What are you doing, Katie?" Jeremy asked with a puzzled face. "I thought we were going for a bike ride." "We are, but—" she hesitated for a moment. "Hey!" said Jeremy suddenly. "Maybe we could just stop in and look at the swing set, Katie! Mom only said we couldn't try it, right?" Katie thought for a minute. "No, Jeremy, we can't do that," she said finally. "That wouldn't really be obeying with our whole hearts. I want to try the swing set, too, but let's honor Mom and the Lord by obeying fully, rather than trying to get as close to disobeying as possible." Jeremy nodded in agreement and with light hearts, they got back on their bikes and headed home, knowing that the Lord was pleased with their decision.

Children, obey your parents in all things, for this is well pleasing to the Lord. (Colossians 3:20)

Do all you can to know Christ,
Read His word and always pray.
Then your desires will be His,
And He will grant them in His way.

"David—here, open this one next!" David's younger brother handed him another gift. The five younger siblings that surrounded him at the dinner table were almost as excited about David's birthday gifts as he was. "Wow! Look, Mom and Dad! Grandpa gave me twenty-five dollars!" David exclaimed. "What are you going to do with all that money?" six-year-old Susan asked with wide eyes. "Well, I don't know just yet, Sue. There are so many things I could use it for, like maybe that new slingshot I've been wanting. What do you think, Dad?" "Well, son, why don't you ask the Lord to show you how to use it." At this, David hesitated. "Okay, Dad, I will." That night as David lay in bed, he started to think about all the ways he could use his birthday money, and then about what his dad had said. "Lord," he prayed, "please show me how you want me to use this money, and please give me a heart that is willing to obey and rejoice in what you ask me to do." The next morning, David found his dad in the living room reading his Bible. "Dad," David started, "I've decided what I want to do with the money." David's father looked up from his Bible in surprise and waited for his son to continue. "I prayed about it like you said, and I thought of the missionary who's been speaking at church. Do you think I could give it to him?" "Son, I'm very proud of you—not for giving away your money, but for asking the Lord to show you how to use it. Yes, I think that is a great way to spend it and I know it will be a wonderful encouragement for him. And actually, it's a good thing you didn't decide to buy the slingshot. I just got a call from your Uncle Steve. He wanted me to tell you that his gift for you is in the mail, and guess what it is?" "A slingshot?!" exclaimed David. His father just smiled.

Delight yourself also in the Lord, And He shall give you the desires of your heart. (Psalm 37:4)

Everything you say and do
Affects how others look at you.
Are you known for doing right
And serving God with all your might?

"Eve, Daniel, Nathan, and Timothy, please listen to me for a moment before we get out of the car. I know you are all very excited about this tour we're about to take through the bakery, but remember, your actions will speak to all those around you even more than your words, so be a good representative for the Lord, alright? You never know who's watching. Okay, let's go!" And with that, Mrs. Morris and her children piled out of the van to join a large group of children and parents for the tour. The Morris children took to heart what their mother had said and endeavored for the next hour to be polite, well-behaved, and interested in what their hosts were showing them, even when those around them were not. When the tour was finished and the Morris's were back in the car and heading home, Mrs. Morris unexpectedly stopped at an ice-cream shop. "Children, I wanted to reward you with a special treat for behaving so well during the tour. I'm very proud of you, but even more importantly, you opened a door for me to share Christ with the bakery manager. She was so impressed by your polite behavior and good attitude that she asked me why you were different from the other children she's seen. I was then able to tell her about our love for the Lord and how we are trying to be good representatives for Him. So you see, even though you're young, the Lord has used your actions to bring His truth to someone else. Good job!"

Even a child is known by his deeds, Whether what he does is pure and right. (Proverbs 20:11)

Fear not, dear child,
For in all things
God's covered you
With angel's wings.

"Faith, are you sure you're ready to sleep in the top bunk?" Faith's mother looked at her doubtfully. "You move a lot in your sleep and if you fall out, it is going to be a long and painful drop to the bottom, especially with our hard floors." "I know, Mama, but I'm ready!" said Faith eagerly, "and besides, you are always reminding us how the Lord watches over us, so I'll be just fine." Faith's mother sighed and said, "That's true, Faith. Alright, if you want to try it, we'll move you up to the top." That night, Faith and her parents gathered to pray before bedtime. Her father ended with, "And Heavenly Father, please watch over Faith tonight as she adjusts to a new bed. Please protect her, Lord. Amen." Faith climbed into bed and was soon fast asleep. Sometime later, Faith began to dream that she was taking a walk in a lovely park. She sat down on a green hillside and noticed a beautiful flower beside her. Leaning over to pick it, she'd just grasped it when—whack! A quick falling sensation ended in an abrupt landing on the floor. Faith woke up with a start and realized that she was on her hands and knees—not on a soft hillside but on the floor of her room. Looking up, she had just realized what had happened when her parents rushed in. "Faith! Are you okay, honey?" Her mother picked her up. "I was so worried this was going to happen! Are you hurt?" Faith carefully moved every limb before announcing, "I'm not hurt at all! I'm not even sore! See, Mama! The Lord did protect me! I even landed on my hands and knees and they're not even red!" "Yes, honey, the Lord did watch over you tonight and I'm so grateful for that," her father said. "However," he added with a twinkle in his eyes, "I think you'll need to move back to the bottom bunk. I don't want to make His angels work overtime!"

For He shall give His angels charge over you, To keep you in all your ways.
(Psalm 91:11)

God gave His Son to die for you
Although you didn't ask Him to,
And greater love you cannot give
Than to give your life so one might live.

"George, did you hear about the MacKenzies?" Mrs. Gerome asked her husband as she spread the picnic blanket on the grass. "Simply unbelievable." "Hear what?" ten-year-old Nick chimed in as he reached for a plate. "Your mother is referring to the missionaries who were taken hostage in the Middle East this week," Mr. Gerome explained as they began to pass around the food. "Why were they captured?" asked Nick with a worried look on his face. "Well," Mr. Gerome began, "because they were telling the people over there about Jesus and many were coming to have faith in Christ, and some people with different beliefs didn't like it." "But why would they even go there if it was so dangerous?" Nick asked, puzzled. "Why couldn't they just write letters or send over Bibles instead?" Mr. Gerome smiled and said, "Nick, God gave those eight missionaries a love for those people and asked them to go over and personally share His love and hope with them in a way that can't always be done with letters. They knew it would be dangerous and that they might even die, but they went anyway. In John 15:13, God tells us that 'Greater love has no one than this, than to lay down one's life for his friends.' Those missionaries risked their lives so that others could spend eternity with the Lord." "Will we all have to do that?" Nick asked hesitantly. "Certainly not," Mr. Gerome said reassuringly, "but even if we don't ever die for Christ, we should spend the time God has given us here on earth sharing His message of salvation with others whenever we have the opportunity. Could you help me remember to do that, son?" "Yes, Dad, I will," Nick said solemnly, "and you can help me remember, too, okay?" "Okay!" said Mr. Gerome. "Now, let's eat this yummy lunch!"

Greater love has no one than this, than to lay down one's life for his friends.
(John 15:13)

How can we have long life
And God's blessing on our days?
We must honor both our parents
In our thoughts and in our ways.

"How does this look?" Maria asked as she walked into her mother's room. "You look lovely dear, and that dress is so becoming," her mother replied. "You look like quite the young lady." "Thanks, Mama," Maria said with a sigh. "Why the sigh, honey?" Maria's mother inquired. "Oh," Maria began, "it's just that some of the other girls at church think it's silly that I always wear a dress to church." "Well," Maria's mother said, "don't worry about them. You are doing what your father and I have asked you to do and that is what is really important. The Lord promises to bless those who honor their parents, and that is exactly what you are doing. And besides, you really do look so feminine and pretty in your dresses. Now, let's head downstairs. I think the rest of the family is waiting to go to church." Shortly thereafter, Maria's family walked into their church. As they made their way toward the meeting room, Maria began to feel embarrassed about her dress as she walked past the other children, but just then, her father looked over at her and said, "Maria, you and your mother look so lovely this morning. No one is going to even notice me and your poor brothers!" A broad smile came over Maria's face at her father's compliment, and she quickly forgot the other children, happy in the knowledge that both her earthly father and Heavenly Father were pleased with her obedience.

Honor your father and your mother, that your days may be long upon the land which the Lord your God is giving you. (Exodus 20:12)

If a task just seems too big
And my strength so very small,
I need only to ask Christ
And He will help me conquer all.

"It's one o'clock, James. Time for you to practice your violin," James' mother called to him from upstairs. James let out a little groan and then slowly walked upstairs. "Why the long face, honey?" James' mother asked. "You usually like practicing." "It's because of the song I'm trying to learn, Mom," James sighed. "It's so hard and I have to be able to play it by next Friday for our recital. I don't think I can do it." "Oh, honey, you've been making good progress! But you know what we're going to do?" "What?" James asked curiously. "We're going to do what we should have done at the very beginning," said his mother while taking his hand. "We're going to ask the Lord to help you conquer this seemingly impossible task, okay?" "Okay, Mom. I'm going to need all the help I can get!" And with that, James and his mother sat down on the couch and prayed, committing James and his music to the Lord and asking Him to help James learn the piece in time for the recital. Each day for the next week, James diligently practiced his violin piece and slowly but surely, he began to master the song. By the evening of the recital, James felt almost ready. "It's my turn to play next, Mom. I'm a little scared!" "I know you are, James, but the Lord has been so faithful to help you this past week, and I know He'll see you through tonight. You'll do great!" As James took his place on stage, he quickly said a prayer, and then proceeded to play his song with almost no mistakes. Afterward his parents congratulated him and he said, "The Lord helped me do it, even when I thought I couldn't! I am so glad He helped me ... and that it's over!"

I can do all things through Christ who strengthens me. (Philippians 4:13)

Jesus loves the little children
And as a father bids them come,
For He knows each of their names
And hears their prayers, every one.

"Jelly?" Thomas asked his little sister as he made sandwiches for lunch. Iris, who was busily working on a project at the table, gave him a distracted "Yes, please." "What are you working on, Sis?" Thomas asked curiously as he handed her a plate. "I'm making a gift for our neighbor, Mrs. White," Iris said looking up. "It's her birthday tomorrow, and she doesn't have any family living here, so I want to cheer her up." Iris quietly returned to her work, but a few minutes later she let out a dismayed cry. "What's wrong?" her mother asked as she walked into the room. "Oh, no!" Iris whimpered. "I ran out of glue, and now I won't be able to finish my gift in time." As Iris started to cry, her mother came over to her and, putting her arm around her said, "Well, since we don't have a way to get more right now, let's stop and ask the Lord to provide some more glue." Thomas let out a laugh. "Isn't that kind of a silly thing to pray for?" he asked. "No person or prayer is ever too small or insignificant in God's eyes, Thomas," his mother said. "God especially loves the simple prayers of children, even for little things." So in saying that, she pulled Iris into her lap, and all three of them prayed. "I feel better, Mama," Iris said as she wiped away her tears. "I know God will help us!" A few hours later, Iris's father arrived home from work. After greeting his wife and children, he handed his wife a plastic bag. "I decided to clean out my desk today," he said. "I brought home a few items you could use here." Iris's eyes met her mother's as she emptied the contents onto the table. Tape, scissors, staples.... "Glue!" Iris shouted and bounced into her father's arms. Iris's father looked at his astounded family with a puzzled expression. "What's going on?" he asked. "You, my dear," said his wife triumphantly, "are an answer to prayer."

Jesus said, "Let the little children come to Me, and do not forbid them; for of such is the kingdom of heaven."
(Matthew 19:14)

Keep a guard over your mouth,
Never let your lips tell lies.
Always speak what's true and right
For the truth needs no disguise.

"Kick the ball to me!" cried Peter excitedly, as he and his brother Mark chased a soccer ball around their backyard. "Boys," their father called out the back door, "please keep the ball out of your mother's flowerbeds. Any damage will have to be repaired during your playtime on Saturday, and after you've been to the hardware store to buy more flowers with your allowance money." "Okay, Dad," answered the boys distractedly as they lined up to try kicking the ball through their tire swing. A few minutes later, Mark said to Peter, "I bet you can't kick the ball onto the roof!" "Yes I can! Watch this!" And with that he gave a mighty kick to the soccer ball, watching with great delight as it flew high into the air, landed on the roof with a thud, and began to roll back down toward them. His delight, however, quickly turned to horror as he realized where the ball was going to land. "Oh, no!" he cried and made a dash for the edge of the house, but it was too late. The ball landed with a thud, right into the middle of his mother's flowerbed. "Look at all those smashed flowers! What am I going to do?" thought Peter to himself. "I could blame it on Mark since he's older and it was his idea. Or I could say that the neighbor dog came dashing through after the ball and did it." "Or—" and at this thought his stomach tightened, "I could tell the truth. I'll be in so much trouble, though!" Peter thought for a second longer, then straightened his shoulders. "No, I want to be a boy of character like the heroes Henty wrote about. And that means I know what I have to do." And with that, Peter walked inside and meekly told his parents what had happened. "Thank you for telling us, Peter, rather than making me cross-examine the two of you about it," his father said. "I appreciate your courage, and although you will still have to replace the flowers, I am very proud of you and I know the Lord is pleased." Peter felt better about it, too.

Keep your tongue from evil, And your lips from speaking deceit. (Psalm 34:14)

Let us always love each other
Just as Christ loves you and me,
Then to the world we'll be a witness
And Christ in us they all will see.

"Luke, have you been over to Mr. Regent's yet to mow his yard?" Mark's father asked as he came down the stairs. "His grass is getting long again." "No," Luke said slowly. "Actually, Dad, I was wondering if I could stop mowing his yard. He never says thank you, and last week he got upset when I mowed too close to his favorite tree. I don't think he likes me very much." "Well, Luke," his father said thoughtfully, "I know Mr. Regent isn't always an easy person to love, but he's also not a Christian. We serve and help him as his neighbor to show him Christ's love, even though he offers nothing to us in return." "Kind of like what Christ did for us, right, Dad?" Luke asked. "Yes, just like that." His father smiled. "Now, do you think you can go and serve him with a joyful heart, even though you probably won't be thanked?" "Yes, Dad, I'll do it!" Luke said as he headed out the door and over to Mr. Regent's with the mower. As he was wheeling it into the driveway, he noticed Mr. Regent's Saturday paper lying beside his mailbox and, remembering his talk with his father, picked it up and carried it to the front door. Ringing the bell, he waited until Mr. Regent had opened the door and then handed him his paper with a smile and said, "Here's your paper, Mr. Regent." The elderly man took it without a word, a look of surprise on his face. Later, as Mark mowed, he looked up once and noticed Mr. Regent watching him from the steps, his newspaper in hand. Luke waved cheerily, and Mr. Regent nodded and briefly raised his hand before going back inside. For the rest of the morning as he mowed, Mark prayed for Mr. Regent, and returned home with a light heart.

Love one another, for love is of God; and everyone who loves is born of God and knows God. (1 John 4:7)

My child, do not judge
By a person's outward fare,
But be as Christ who looks inside
To see what's really there.

"Mom, what's wrong with that new boy in our home-school group?" Samuel asked one morning. "You mean Nathan Johnson?" Samuel's mother replied. "He was in a car accident when he was little, and now has to use a wheelchair." "Will he get better?" Samuel questioned. "He might. Why?" "Well," Samuel began, "because the other kids won't play with him because he can't get around very well. So I was hoping that maybe he'd get better so he wouldn't be different anymore." "I see," his mother said thoughtfully. "Samuel, the Lord has allowed Nathan to have a special outward challenge in his life, but that doesn't mean he's any different inwardly. Inside, he's just like you. He has an imagination and loves to read and talk and play. Have you ever tried getting to know him?" "I guess not," Samuel said slowly. "But what about the other kids? They won't understand."

"Samuel," his mother looked at him seriously, "what the other kids do or think is not important. What is important is what the Lord tells us, and in 1 Samuel, the book of the Bible you were named after, He tells us not to judge a person by their outward appearance. I want you to ask the Lord to show you how He sees Nathan, alright?" "Alright, Mom," replied Samuel. A few days later, Samuel announced to his mother, "Mom, you were right!" "About what?" she laughed. "I spent a whole hour talking with Nathan today, and he is so smart!" Samuel said in awe. "He's going to show me next week how to use his telescope so we can watch a comet that will be passing overhead!" "Good job, Samuel," his mother said with a smile.

...[M]an looks at the outward appearance, but the Lord looks at the heart. (1 Samuel 16:7)

Never stray away
From the pathways of the Lord,
Listen to His words
And with blessings He'll reward.

"Noodles and pasta sauce?" "Check!" Chris answered his mother's question. "Milk and eggs?" Mrs. Pentland asked next. "Got it!" replied her daughter Natalie. "Okay, let's see what else we need from the store while we're here," Mrs. Pentland said as she looked at her list. "Natalie, can you go get some bananas while we head over to the deli?" "Yes, Ma'am!" Natalie said as she headed off toward the other end of the store. Natalie had just put the bananas into a plastic bag when she noticed a woman next to her drop something as she pulled a grocery list from her purse. Hesitating for a minute as she waited for the woman to notice, Natalie watched in surprise as the woman turned and walked toward a different aisle. Walking over to the fallen object, Natalie picked it up and stifled a gasp as she unfolded it. "A fifty dollar bill!" she exclaimed under her breath. "Hooray! Finder's keepers!" But her rejoicing was short-lived for just then her conscience began to bother her. Finally she thought, "I need to give this back. Keeping it would be wrong, and I don't want to displease you, Lord. Forgive me for hesitating." So with that, Natalie went to search for the rightful owner. When Natalie found her, she tapped her lightly on the shoulder and said, "Ma'am, I saw this drop from your purse and wanted to return it to you." The lady looked at Natalie in astonishment as she received the money back. "Why, thank you," she stammered. "This is my grocery money and I didn't even realize I'd dropped it!" Natalie just smiled and started to walk away when the lady called her back. "Young lady," she said, "here is five dollars. It's all I can spare right now, but may the Lord bless you in some other way." "Thank you!" Katie said as she again turned to leave. "And thank you, Lord," she said quietly, "for helping me do what was right."

Now therefore, listen to me, my children, For blessed are those who keep my ways. (Proverbs 8:32)

O children, praise the Lord,
Tell others of His ways,
And though you may be small,
Your words will bring Him praise!

"O kay children, it's time for dinner," said Mr. Oliver. "I'm sure your grandparents are hungry, so let's all sit down." As he said this, the Oliver children, along with Mrs. Oliver and her parents, gathered around the dinner table. Once everyone was seated, Mr. Oliver asked the family to bow their heads as he blessed the meal. Most of the children didn't notice that Mrs. Oliver's father hadn't closed his eyes, except for little Joy who had peeked between her fingers. As the different dishes were passed around, Joy became more and more fidgety until finally, amidst the chatter at the table she asked, "Grandpa, why don't you close your eyes when you pray?" An uncomfortable silence followed before her grandfather replied, "Because, Joy, I don't pray." Joy's eyes widened in shock and she asked, "Why? Don't you like talking to Jesus?" Her grandfather answered, "I don't pray, Joy, because I don't know if I believe in

Jesus." "Oh, Grandpa," Joy said as her voice quivered, "Who takes care of you? He always watches over me, and loves me even when I'm bad, and I am going to go to heaven when I die. Oh, Grandpa, please believe! I want you to go to heaven, too!" Everyone was silent for a moment, and then, to Mrs. Oliver's amazement, her father said quietly, "I have been bad, too, Joy. I don't think Jesus could love me like He loves you." "Oh, yes He could, Grandpa!" said Joy with enthusiasm. "He loves everyone!" "Well, Joy," said her grandfather with watery eyes, "I'll think about what you said, okay?" "Alright, Grandpa," Joy said, "and I'll be praying for you, but don't wait too long! I have to go to bed at eight!"

Out of the mouth of babes and nursing infants You have ordained strength, Because of Your enemies, That You may silence the enemy and the avenger.
(Psalm 8:2)

Pass on kind and pleasant words
To those in need of cheer,
For as you do they'll cheer you too
And will dry up many a tear.

"Paddle to the left, Peter! Quick!" Paul cried to his little brother as a big rock came into view around a bend in the river, splitting the water in half and causing a loud gushing noise as the water cascaded off a small drop. Along the right side of the rock, the water poured over a steep drop-off that ended in more rocks. On the left side, their only safe option, the water flowed down a gentler but swift incline to the lower riverbed. Peter switched his paddle to the other side of the canoe as quickly as he could and began to paddle with all his might. "I can't do it, Paul!" he cried in despair as the rock came closer. "Yes you can, Peter!" Paul shouted encouragingly to him. "I know you can! I'm helping you, too. Just keep paddling!" Slowly their canoe began to turn, and just as they were approaching the rock, the nose of the canoe cleared the dangerous obstacle, and they rushed down the left side. "Whew, that was close!" Paul grinned as he splashed a little water in Peter's direction. "Good work, little bro! See? You did great! I think I've got the best canoe partner out here!" "Really?" Peter beamed at his older brother. "Thanks, Paul!" he replied, and before Paul could warn him, Peter had jumped up and started toward Paul to give him a hug. "Wait, Peter! Don't stand up!" Paul started to object. "You'll tip the—whoa!" And with a big splash, both boys fell out of the canoe and into the water. Surfacing, the two drug the canoe to the side of the river and stood up. "I'm sorry, Paul!" Peter said as he hung his head. Wringing the water out of his shirt, Paul laughed and said, "Hey, little bro, don't worry about it. I was hot anyway. And I still have the best canoe partner!" Looking up, Peter smiled and gave Paul a big hug that knocked them both back into the water.

Pleasant words are like a honeycomb, Sweetness to the soul and health to the bones.
(Proverbs 16:24)

Quietly rest as you wait on the Lord
And remember that you're in His care,
Then fearlessly do what He asks you to do
And the badge of His courage you'll wear.

"Quickly, Thomas, grab your coat and come outside with me," his mother said as she opened the front door. "The goats have gotten out of the pen and with the storm coming, I'm afraid some of them will be lost." Thomas put on his coat and stepped outside into the wind, looking doubtfully at the darkening sky. He didn't like storms, but he liked the ornery goats even less. Following close behind his mother, he saw their six goats scattered in a small field just beyond their pen. "I'll round up Missy and the other females," Thomas's mother said through the wind. "I need you to get Old Bastion. He's very important." Thomas's eyes grew wide with horror as he looked toward the large billy goat standing at the far edge of the field. "But, Mother—" he started to object, but his mother was already pulling one of the goats toward the pen. "Father," Thomas prayed as he slowly walked toward Old Bastion, "Please help me! Protect me and help me to complete this task bravely for my mother." A quiet confidence slowly filled him as he approached the goat who was eyeing him warily. He stood facing the old goat for a minute when an idea suddenly came to him. Pulling from his pocket a piece of apple that he'd stuffed there earlier, he held it out toward Old Bastion. To his amazement, the goat slowly began to walk toward him, took the apple out of his hand, and munched happily as Thomas grabbed his collar and led him back into the pen. Both Thomas and his mother sighed with relief as the pen door was closed, and they returned to their warm home just as the storm was breaking. "Thank you, Thomas, for your bravery. I know how much you dislike that old goat." "Thank you Lord," Thomas whispered, "for making me brave!"

...in quietness and in confidence shall be your strength... (Isaiah 30:15)

Remember, dear child,
The One up above
Who's given you life
And shown you His love.

"Ready, set, jump!" Mr. Hayden shouted as his two sons jumped off the wheelbarrow and into the pile of leaves he'd been collecting. The boys laughed as they rolled down the side of the pile, leaves flying everywhere and sticking out of their hair and clothes. "Isn't it beautiful out here, boys?" Mr. Hayden asked as Matthew and Caleb stood up and brushed themselves off. "I love autumn, with its colorful leaves and crisp, cool air. God has created such an amazing world for us to enjoy, hasn't He?" The boys nodded their hearty approval. "What are your favorite things about fall, Matthew?" Mr. Hayden asked. Thinking a moment, Matthew replied, "I think it's all the fun things that fall brings, like warm fires, hot cocoa, and Thanksgiving!" Mr. Hayden laughed and said, "I agree! Now what about you, Caleb?" Without hesitation, Caleb jumped up and shouted "leaf fights!" and began throwing leaves at his dad and brother. For the next

five minutes, all three engaged in a furious leaf fight. Finally, collapsing into an exhausted heap of laughter, Mr. Hayden waited to catch his breath and then said, "Everything—from the seasons, to the beautiful mountains, oceans, and rivers, to the many different types of plants and animals God has placed here on Earth with us—all speak of both God's amazing creativity as well as His love for us. Matthew, Caleb—it is so important that you love and follow Christ whole-heartedly even now while you are young, and that you always serve Him with a grateful heart for all that He has done for you. Each time you enjoy this marvelous creation God has placed us in, thank Him, both for this life and the even more beautiful life that is to come. In fact, let's do that right now." So amidst the colorful leaves and cool autumn breeze, all three knelt down and gave thanks to the Lord.

Remember now your Creator in the days of your youth. (Ecclesiastes 12:1)

Stand guard, O lips!
Let no ill words pass through.
O Lord, help me
To say what's good and true!

"Stop!" Juan cried as he watched his younger brother aim his plastic crossbow at the model airplane Juan had just built ... but it was too late. There was a great crash as the airplane took a "bullet" and fell off the table. "Alex!" yelled Juan. "You little tornado! What are you doing!" He was going to say more, but just then his grandfather came into the room. "My my, what is going on in here?" he asked, looking at the boys. Alex made a dash for the door, leaving Juan standing there amidst the ruins of his plane. "Grandpa, Alex just destroyed my airplane with his crossbow! Look at it! The pieces are everywhere." He looked sadly at the wreckage and then stamped his foot. "He makes me so angry sometimes! I know he does it just to upset me!" "And it looks like he's doing a good job of it," his grandfather smiled. "What did you just call him? A 'little tornado'?" Juan shrugged and looked at the floor. "Juan," his grandfather continued, "I'm sure your parents have said this before, but you must be careful to guard what comes out of your mouth, even when you are angry." His grandfather reached down to pick up one of Juan's toy soldiers and held it in front of him. "You see this soldier? He is told to guard the gate of the Castillo at all costs, but what happens if he fails?" Juan thought a moment. "Those inside will get hurt," he said. "Yes," said his grandfather, "And just like this soldier, you must learn to guard your mouth, or you will end up saying something that will hurt someone else. A true Christian soldier does what is right, regardless of what others do to him. Will you trust the Lord to teach you that?" "Yes, Grandpa," Juan said resolutely. "I will be a good soldier and guard my mouth ... and I am sorry I called Alex a 'little tornado.'" His grandfather smiled and said, "Now, let's find some superglue."

Set a guard, O Lord, over my mouth;
Keep watch over the door of my lips.
(Psalm 141:3)

There is one thing you must do
To keep your witness bright,
You must love the Lord your God
With all your heart and soul and might!

"This hill looks kind of steep, Karen!" Ashley said as they scooted up to the edge of the hill with their sled. "Oh, it will be fun!" Karen giggled as she settled herself at the front. Ashley gave one last doubtful look at the bottom and jumped on the back behind her twin sister. "One, two, THREE!" Karen shouted and pushed off. Down they flew over the side of the hill, screaming and laughing as they bounced along at lightning speed. As they came to the bottom, the sled skidded to a stop and both girls fell off into the soft snow with a laugh. "That was fun!" Ashley said as they stood up to brush themselves off. "Look how far down we came! That hill looks so big from here." "Yep! I knew you could do it," Karen said as they started back up the hill. Suddenly, the girls heard their father's voice calling them. Turning, they saw him waiting for them by their gate down below and hurried down to him. "Hi, Daddy!"

they said as they came up to him. "Looks like you two are having fun," their father smiled. "I noticed, though, that in all your hurry to get out here, you skipped your Bible time. Is that right?" he asked. They both looked at him sheepishly. "Girls, I know how much you love to sled and that is wonderful, but you need to be sure you don't let it push aside building your relationship with the Lord. The time you spend with Him is the most important thing, okay?" "Yes, Daddy, I'm sorry," Karen said quietly. "Me, too," Ashley echoed. "Well," their father continued, "How about you come in for some hot chocolate and Bible time, and then come back out to sled." "Okay!" the girls exclaimed together as they all headed for the house.

...thou shalt love the Lord thy God with all thine heart, and with all thy soul, and with all thy might... (Deuteronomy 6:5)

Up and down my life may take me,
I'll have days both good and bad.
But no matter where I'm going,
Keep my steps, Lord, in Your paths.

"Up, up, up!" Mrs. Mayburn said as she threw open the curtains on her daughter's window. "You've overslept and we have lots to do today to get ready for our trip." "I don't feel very good, Mom," Cecelia said, sitting up. Her mother felt her forehead. "You are a little warm. Well, maybe you'll feel better as you start moving." Cecelia drug herself out of bed and headed to the bathroom. After five exasperating minutes of looking for her toothbrush, she suddenly found it in the bathtub where her little sister had been using it for a dog brush. "Ugh!" she muttered as she headed back to her room to find something to wear. Putting on her favorite shirt, she discovered that an unexplained laundry accident had left a bleach mark on the front. Now, close to tears, she threw on something else and headed downstairs for breakfast. As she sat down, her father said, "Cecelia, you left the popcorn bowl in the living room last night and since then, Muffins has dumped the leftovers all over the carpet. You'll need to clean that up." "But it wasn't—" Cecelia began to protest but her father interrupted. "Now, no excuses, alright? Just clean it up." At this, Cecelia finally burst into tears. Alarmed, her father said, "Honey, it's not that difficult is it? I'm not upset with you!" Between sobs Cecelia explained her awful morning to her father. "Ah, I see," he said sympathetically. "I'm sorry this has been a hard morning. Sometimes we're going to have difficult days, but you know what the important thing is?" "What?" Cecelia asked, drying her eyes. "That we thank the Lord for both the good and the bad, even though it is hard, and ask Him to help us respond to our trials as He would want us to. Can you try that today?" Cecelia nodded to her father as he continued, "Good! Now, let's start this morning over shall we?" And with that he gave her a big hug.

Uphold my steps in Your paths, That my footsteps may not slip. (Psalm 17:5)

Very little it may be,
The helping hand that comes from me,
But though I'm small, you, Lord, will see
The way I serve as unto Thee.

"Vacuuming will be your job, Jonathan and Mark. Caleb and Thomas, you can help Daddy and Mr. Dowring set up the chairs, alright?" Mrs. Berg looked at her sons as they nodded and hurried off. "Girls, let's head to the kitchen and see what help Mrs. Dowring needs." With that, Mrs. Berg and her daughters headed for the large kitchen at the back of the one-room shelter for the homeless. Around the edge of the room were cots for sleeping, and a small podium and chalkboard stood in a corner, just below a sign that read, "Welcome to Agape House." In the center of the room were tables decorated with Thanksgiving napkins and plates and small pumpkins. As they entered the kitchen, Lydia, the youngest Berg, looked up at her mother and asked, "Mama, what can I do?" Mrs. Dowring, the shelter's cook, overheard her and said, "I have a very special job for you." Lydia's eyes got very big as she said eagerly, "What?" "I need you to help me put these rolls into the baskets," Mrs. Dowring said as she placed the bread on a low table. "They need to look very pretty and neat. Do you think you can do that?" "Yes!" Lydia said excitedly and began to work on her project. For the next several hours, the Dowrings, Bergs, and other volunteers prepared and served a delicious Thanksgiving dinner to the one hundred people that came, with Mr. Dowring, the shelter's director, closing the evening by inviting the attendees to stay and sing a few hymns. On the way home, all the children agreed that this was the best Thanksgiving they'd ever had. "Your rolls looked so nice in the baskets," Mr. Berg said to Lydia, "and all of you did such a wonderful job. We all have so much to be thankful for." Everyone agreed.

Verily I say unto you, Inasmuch as ye have done it unto one of the least of these my brethren, ye have done it unto me. (Matthew 25:40)

When dark shadows on the wall
Or noises strange make me feel small,
I'll not fear but trust in You
And know that you'll protect me, too.

"Whew, ten o'clock! It's been a busy day!" Abby's father smiled. "And it's way past your bedtime! Now hop into bed and we'll pray." Abigail jumped into her bed and snuggled under the sheets. Taking her father's hand, she closed her eyes as he began to pray. "Our Father, thank you for granting us this day. Thank you for your Son, Jesus Christ, whom you sent to save us and give us eternal life. And now, Father, I ask that you would watch over Abigail tonight as she sleeps. Amen." Abigail echoed her own amen, gave her father a hug, and soon drifted off to sleep. A few hours later, Abigail woke with a start. "Boom!" A great flash of lightning lit up her room, followed by a huge crash. Abigail quickly pulled the covers over her head and wrapped her arms around her stuffed bunny. "I'm so scared!" she thought. "What should I do?" She wanted to go to her parent's room, but that seemed so far away, and she couldn't stay under the sheets forever because it was getting too hot. "Lord," she prayed, "please help me! I'm so afraid! Please watch over me and give me peace. Thank you, Lord." Abigail, feeling a little better, slowly pulled the sheets from over her head and began reciting in her mind all the Bible verses she could remember. Soon, despite the continuing storm, her eyes drooped closed and she fell fast asleep. She didn't wake up again until the sun peeped through her window, telling her that a new day had dawned. "Thank you, Lord," she whispered, "for taking care of me. Next time, I won't be so afraid!"

Whenever I am afraid, I will trust in You. (Psalm 56:3)

Trust in the Lord with all thine heart; and lean not unto thine own understanding. PROVERBS 3:5

Except I do all as to You Lord
And look to You for my reward,
Then all my work and time is vain;
I need not waste the toil nor pain.

X "Exactly where are you taking my good sewing scissors?" Isaac's mother asked him as he was opening the patio door. "I'm going to use them to cut the rope I need for my tree house!" he said, looking at his mother tentatively. "Oh, no you don't," she said, holding her hand out for them. Isaac handed them over reluctantly. "Isaac, your father is in the garage. Why don't you go ask him to help you. Building a tree house is a big job, and I'm sure he'd love to help you." "No, it's okay, Mom. I can do it! I know just where I'm going to put it!" And with that he ran out the door. For the next several hours, Isaac's mother and father watched him haul boards from the garage to a big oak tree in their backyard, cut rope, and hammer nail after nail into his treehouse frame. His mother was just getting ready to call Isaac in for lunch when they heard a big *crash* come from the backyard. Running outside, his parents found him sitting on a pile of twisted boards, crying. "What happened? Are you alright?" his father asked as he picked him up. He held Isaac until his crying subsided. Then Isaac began to explain what happened. "I had finished the floor of my treehouse and was climbing up to try it when the whole thing fell down! All my work is ruined." "Isaac," his father began, "I would have loved to help you with your treehouse if you'd only asked me. I know we could build a really great treehouse together, if you'd just ask. You know, this is kind of like our lives," he continued. "When we try to do something on our own without asking for the Lord's help, we make mistakes and usually end up wasting lots of time and money, when all we have to do is ask the Lord for His help." He was quiet for a moment and then Isaac said softly, "Dad, could you help me build a treehouse?" "Of course, son, I'd love to!" His father said, giving him a big hug. "In fact, we'll get started right after we eat lunch, okay?" "Okay!" Isaac cheered as they turned to go inside.

Except the Lord build the house, they labor in vain who build it. (Psalm 127:1)

You dear little ones, God's lambs so sweet,
Rejoice for you'll not know defeat!
If you are Christ's, the victory's won
And sin and death are overcome!

"You naughty lamb," Gracie murmured as she walked through the brush. "Where are you?" "Find anything?" asked Charles, Gracie's older brother, as he emerged from the trees. "Wait!" he said suddenly. "Listen." In the distance, a very faint bleating could be heard. "There!" Charles said triumphantly. Hurrying toward the sound, the children came to a steep drop-off. Looking over the edge, they saw the lamb a few feet below on a small ledge. "Poor thing!" Gracie said compassionately. "How did you get down there?" Charles was about to jump down after it when they were startled by a low growl. Whirling around, they found themselves staring at a large mountain lion. The mountain lion looked at them warily and then, hearing the lamb, began to walk toward them. "What should we do, Charles?" Gracie whispered in a panicked voice. Quickly Charles prayed, "Lord, give us courage and show us what to do!" "Gracie," he said quietly, "climb down onto the ledge with the lamb and stay there." Gracie instantly obeyed. Then, turning around, Charles locked eyes with the mountain lion. The creature, sensing the challenge, growled fiercely and began to crouch. Charles backed up until only his toes were still on the edge of the cliff and waited. Suddenly, with lightning speed, the mountain lion sprung at him. With only a split second before impact with the cat, Charles let his toes slip off the edge of the cliff and fell onto the ledge below with Gracie and the lamb. The mountain lion flew off the cliff only a few feet above their heads and plummeted to the bottom of the canyon. "Oh, Charles," Gracie said as she burst into tears. "It's alright," he said gently. "The Lord has delivered us from our enemy and protected this little lamb. God has helped us to overcome! Now, let's take this lost lamb back to the flock."

You are of God, little children, and have overcome them, because He who is in you is greater than he who is in the world. (1 John 4:4)

Zion rejoices in truth, O Lord,
And so shall we give thanks
That your judgments are just
And in You we can trust
And that heaven will be our reward.

"Zip up your jacket, Emma. It's going to be chilly out there this morning!" Emma obeyed her Aunt Barbara's instructions as they headed out to the barn to saddle up the horses. It was early morning and the sun was just beginning to thaw the white frost that softly covered the grass and fenceposts. Something in the air this morning told them that winter was on its way. Aunt Barbara and Emma mounted their horses and then started out down a trail leading across the pasture and away from the house. Emma loved it when her family came to visit her aunt on her farm, and this morning's trail ride was a special reward to Emma for memorizing the first chapter of James. For several minutes, Emma enjoyed just looking around at the few dairy cows that grazed around them and listening to the birds that had braved the cold to welcome the day with their song. They rode through a thick forest, and several times stopped to watch deer and even a small bear that wandered across the path ahead of them. Finally, as they came around a bend, Emma could see that the trees ended but she couldn't see around her aunt's horse to what was beyond them. Pulling her horse off to the side, her aunt stopped and allowed Emma to come up beside her. Stopping her horse, Emma gasped as she looked out across a beautiful canyon stretching out below them. "It's beautiful!" Emma exclaimed. "I don't think I've ever seen anything so pretty! What a special reward this was! Thank you!" "And you know what is so amazing, Emma?" her aunt said quietly. "Our heavenly reward is going to be a hundred times better!" "Wow," Emma said. "I can't wait!" "Me either, Emma," her aunt replied. "Me either."

Zion hears and is glad ... because of Your judgments, O Lord. (Psalm 97:8)

OTHER BOOKS *from* VISION FORUM

The Adventure of Missionary Heroism

Be Fruitful and Multiply

Beloved Bride

The Bible Lessons of John Quincy Adams for His Son

The Birkenhead Drill

The Boy's Guide to the Historical Adventures of G.A. Henty

Christian Modesty and the Public Undressing of America

Coming In on a Wing and a Prayer

Destination: Moon

The Elsie Dinsmore Series

Family Man, Family Leader

Home-Making

How God Wants Us to Worship Him

The Letters and Lessons of Teddy Roosevelt for His Sons

The Life and Campaigns of Stonewall Jackson

Little Faith

Missionary Patriarch

Mother

The New-England Primer

Of Plymouth Plantation

The Original Blue Back Speller

Poems for Patriarchs

Safely Home

Sergeant York and the Great War

So Much More

The Sinking of the Titanic

Ten P's in a Pod

Thoughts for Young Men

To Have and to Hold

Verses of Virtue